T0207693

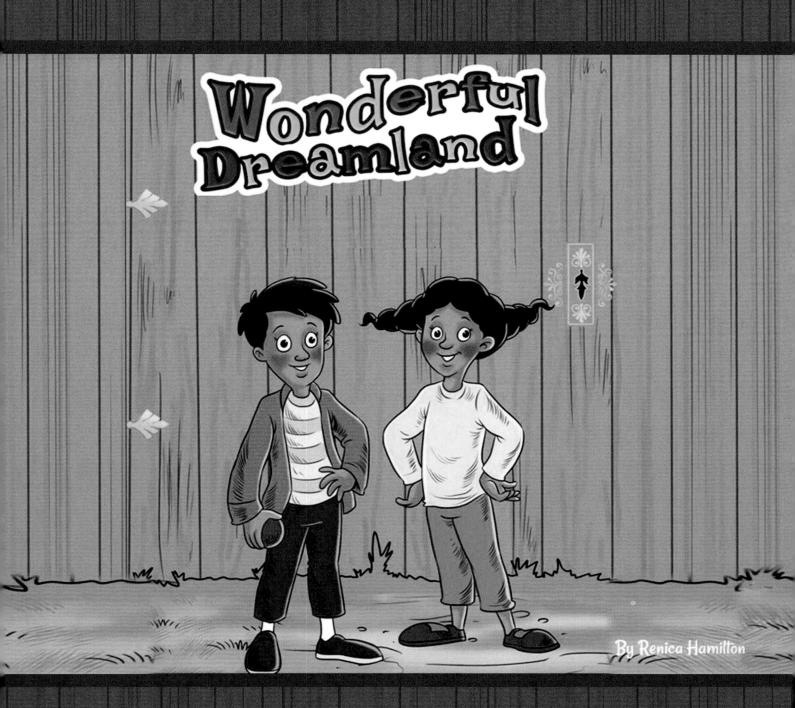

Order this book online at www.trafford.com
or email orders@trafford.com

Most Trafford titles are also available at major online book retailers.

 www.trafford.com

North America & international
toll-free: 844 688 6899 (USA & Canada)
fax: 812 355 4082

Our mission is to efficiently provide the world's finest, most comprehensive book publishing
service, enabling every author to experience success. To find out how to publish your book,
your way, and ha ve it available worldwide, visit us online at www.trafford.com

ISBN: 978-1-6987-0556-9 (sc)

Print information available on the last page.

Trafford rev.01/26/2021

There once was a town far, far away, where the people would laugh and the children would play. This town was hidden from the rest of the world to see. The only way in was to have the town key. Dreamland was the name of this town full of treasure; so full of peace, love, joy and pleasure.

The fun and excitement would last all day as the good people of Dreamland would constantly say: "Blessings and blessings all around! We are so fortunate to be in this town!"

Everything was perfect, as perfect could be; even the hill with the perfect tree. It was on this hill that the children would play; running and rolling everyday. One day on this hill, Lilly and Rich played ball. Rich was not looking and he let the ball fall.

Fast down the hill, the ball rolled. Rich was relieved when the ball hit a pole. But then the ball bounced high in the air. Rich could not find the ball anywhere.

"Up there in the sky!" yelled Lilly to Rich. He opened his arms for the ball to catch. Drop, drop, bounce swish! Rich tried to catch the ball, but he missed. The ball continued to roll once more. It kept rolling and rolling then went out of the town door.

"Oh no!" yelled Lilly and Rich in shock, for they knew it was nearing time for the town to lock. "I think we can make it." Said Lilly to Rich; but they did not know the ball fell into a ditch. They did not know what was beyond the town door. There was a whole new world for Lilly and Rich to explore.

Finally, they found what they were looking for, so they headed back towards the town door. They noticed the town door was sealed tight. They cried and trembled, filled with fright; "We do not have a key to get back in. We do not belong here, we belong in Dreamland!" All of a sudden, they heard a noise. They looked on the ground at what looked like little toys.

They searched here and there and everywhere for the ball; so focused on finding it that they missed the town call. "Dreamland will close by the count of three. If you need to get in, then you must use your key! One, one, in you should come. Two, two, we're waiting on you! Three, three, too late use your key!"

The little creatures scattered about to and fro, rushing as if they had somewhere to go.

Lilly said to Rich, "Toys! Let's play!" They were surprised to hear one of the little creatures say, "We are not toys, we are tiny girls and boys, who like you one day, got locked out of town. Our worlds were turned completely around."

"Each day before the night would fall, we would notice ourselves shrink and get small. The reason we got smaller everyday, was because the memories of us were fading away. Now we need your help to get back in. You must get into Dreamland and remember us again!"

"Oh no!" said Lilly, "Can't you see? We can't get back in, we do not have the town key!" The tiny girls and boys began to smile, for they had been waiting for this moment all the while. You see, they were the reason the ball fell into a ditch. They needed the help of Lilly and Rich.

"We have a plan to get you back in, and once you are in, you can remember us again. Before the night falls, we need to flatten out your ball. Let the air out and stretch it out tall. Then lay it flat upon this tree, and we will make ourselves into the town key."

They wrapped themselves up in the ball really tight and made a town key that would fit just right! Rich used the key and opened the door. He was so excited to see Dreamland once more! Lilly said to Rich, "We have one more thing to do. Remember the tiny girls and boys so they can enjoy Dreamland too!"

Just in that moment, Lilly and Rich could see, the tiny girls and boys were back to the way they used to be. They laughed and played for the rest of the day. Throughout the night, they continued to say: "Blessings and blessings, all around! We are so fortunate to be back in this town!"